BiLLY BONKERS

It's a CRAZY CHRISTMAS!

With special thanks to Rachel Elliot

G.A.

ORCHARD BOOKS
338 Euston Road, London NW1 3BH
Orchard Books Australia
Level 17/207 Kent Street, Sydney, NSW 2000

First published in 2014 by Orchard Books

ISBN 978 1 40830 054 1

Text © Giles Andreae 2014
Cover artwork © Spike Gerrell 2014
Interior artwork © Spike Gerrell 2014

A CIP catalogue record for this book is available from the British Library.

1 3 5 7 9 10 8 6 4 2

Printed in Great Britain

Orchard Books is a division of Hachette Children's Books,
an Hachette UK company.

www.hachette.co.uk

BILLY BONKERS

It's a CRAZY CHRISTMAS!

Giles Andreae
Illustrated by Spike Gerrell

ORCHARD

Giles Andreae is an award-winning children's author who has written many bestselling picture books, including *Giraffes Can't Dance* and *Commotion in the Ocean*.

He is also the creator of the phenomenally successful Purple Ronnie, Britain's favourite stick man. Giles lives by the river near Oxford with his wife and four young children.

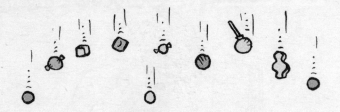

Contents

It's Raining Sweets!

"Lordy lorks, what are you doing?"

Mrs Bonkers glared at the round, wobbly bottom that was poking out of the cupboard under the stairs. She jabbed it with her finger, and heard a muffled yelp.

"Come out of there at once!" she said.

The bottom wiggled from side to side and

then slowly reversed out of the cupboard. Finally the tousled head of William Benedict Bertwhistle Bonkers appeared. He blinked up at his mother and gave a nervous smile.

"Well?" she demanded.

William – or Billy, as he preferred to be called – told himself to think fast. Mrs Bonkers' arms were folded and her right fluffy slipper was tapping on the floor. These were not good signs.

"I...er...well, you see..."

His brain obviously wasn't getting the message about thinking fast.

"You can forget about the Christmas sweets," said his mother. "You won't find them this year."

Billy was starting to worry that she was right. He had usually found them, snaffled some and hidden the wrappers by now.

Where could Mrs Bonkers have hidden them? Their house wasn't that big, and as far as he knew there were no secret passages.

Were there?

Billy looked at his mum's frown and decided to look again later. Mrs Bonkers was under a bit of stress. Not only was half the Bonkers family staying with them for Christmas, but Mr Bonkers had invited all the neighbours to a fireworks party tomorrow night. She marched back into the kitchen, and there was a whiff of burnt mince pies as she closed the door.

Billy sighed longingly. Most people prefer their mince pies to be golden brown.

Not Billy. He liked them just the way Mrs Bonkers always made them – somewhere between charred and incinerated.

His sister, Betty, poked her head around the sitting-room door. "Billy, come and help me put some more decorations up," she said. "I've found a place where Dad hasn't stashed fireworks."

Billy shut the cupboard door and hurried into the sitting room. He and Betty loved Christmas.

They always chose the biggest tree and the shiniest baubles. But this year it was difficult to find a place for the decorations among the towering piles of fireworks that Mr Bonkers had collected. Not to mention the fact that there was a Bonkers family member in every seat.

Billy wasn't very good at remembering the names of relatives he hardly ever saw. So he had drawn himself a reminder picture, which he kept in his pocket, away from prying eyes.

WILBERFORCE BONKERS

Family tree: Second cousin
Top skills: 1. Being a goody two-shoes. 2. His mum thinks he sings like an angel. (She's wrong.)

GREAT UNCLE HERBERT BONKERS

Family tree: Dad's uncle – Wilberforce's grandad
Top skill: Delivering chokingly stinky farts that can clear a room in three seconds flat.

GREAT AUNT MILLIE BONKERS

Family tree: Dad's aunt – Wilberforce's granny
Top skill: Getting her own way. (Note: Ask for tips.)

PATRICIA BONKERS

Family tree: Wilberforce's mum
Top skill: Boasting about Wilberforce.

COLIN BONKERS

Family tree: Dad's cousin – Wilberforce's dad
Top skill: Unknown. (Still waiting for him to say more than two words at a time.)

AUNT ABBIE BONKERS

Family tree: Dad's sister
Top skills: 1. Giving makeovers. 2. Turning her eyelids inside out.

"This is going to be the best fireworks Christmas party this street has ever seen," Mr Bonkers was saying. "Roger Rocket is going to be so jealous he'll eat his own bow tie!"

Cousin Wilberforce smoothed down his neat hair.

"I like bow ties," he said. "Mr Rocket sounds like a very well-dressed man."

Wilberforce's mum, Patricia, gave a proud giggle.

"Wilberforce knows all about designer fashion," she said. "He is always giving his classmates tips on how to dress better. If he wasn't going to be a talented, famous singer, he would make a talented, famous fashion designer."

"I'm going to enter Britain's Super Singers next year and share my talent with the world," said Wilberforce.

There was a long silence while everyone thought about this. As he balanced on one leg between a box of crackling comets and a vase of extra-long sparklers to reach the Christmas tree, Billy tried to decide  what was worse: Great Uncle Herbert's farts, or the fact that he had to share his bedroom with Wilberforce.

"What a wonderful child," said Mr Bonkers, clearing his throat.

Billy wasn't a genius like Wilberforce, but he had a sneaky feeling that Mr Bonkers wasn't quite as impressed as he sounded.

"I've almost got it all planned out," Mr Bonkers went on. "I'm just working out how to set off the sky rockets in time with the music."

"Nigel, dear, the local hardware shop has a special offer on hard hats," said Mrs Bonkers, who had just walked in. "I might just pop down and pick up a few dozen for our guests."

"Nonsense, balderdash and piffle," said Mr Bonkers. "Perfectly safe. Fireworks of the century."

Ever since Bonfire Night, the whole street had been talking about Mr Rocket's amazing fireworks display. Mr Bonkers had talked about it a lot too. He had said things like, "Wasn't that impressive," "The street's gone mad," and "Could do better myself," but no one else seemed to agree with him.

Billy loved helping his dad with his latest plans, and this one sounded as if it was going to be brilliant. While he was looking at the fireworks plans, he forgot all about the Christmas sweets. But at bedtime, as he watched Wilberforce brush his hair

and fold up his hanky, Billy's stomach gnawed with longing. He hadn't tasted a single sneaky marshmallow sparkle fudge whirl, and he felt that he might not make it to Christmas Day without one. He tried to take his mind off sweets by thinking about the mystery that was Wilberforce.

Wilberforce had said "no thank you" to all mince pies and biscuits. He had shown immaculate table manners and filled up the dishwasher without being asked.

He had played chess with his father and emptied the washing machine for Mrs Bonkers. Twice. Was it really possible that they were related?

You probably know by now that Billy

is very good at sleeping. An alarm clock strapped to each ear wouldn't wake him in the middle of the night. So when his eyes flicked open at three a.m., he knew that something funny was going on. He listened for a moment. At first, everything seemed quiet. Then he heard it.

RUSTLE

It was very faint, but if there was one thing that Billy could hear from half a mile away...

RUSTLE RUSTLE

...it was the sound of someone opening a marshmallow sparkle fudge whirl.

RUSTLE RUSTLE RUSTLE

He had to find out where it was coming from! Billy swung his legs over the edge of his bed and tiptoed out onto the landing. The noise was even louder now. It was coming from downstairs.

RUSTLE   RUSTLE   *RUSTLE*

Billy's tummy gurgled. After all, I expect you'll agree that it's never too late to eat sweets. He tiptoed down the stairs, pausing after every step to listen.

"The kitchen," he whispered to himself.

At that moment, Billy wasn't thinking about all the people who were asleep in the house. He wasn't wondering why someone was snaffling sweets in the kitchen. He didn't even consider that it might be a burglar. All he cared about was getting hold of a marshmallow sparkle fudge whirl before they all disappeared. He thundered down the rest of the stairs, sprinted along the hallway and skidded across the kitchen floor. He crashed into a pile of golden, rustling sweet wrappers, lost his footing and fell flat on his back. And that's when he realised that he was staring up at the chocolate-covered face of cousin Wilberforce.

"YOU!" Billy said with a gasp.

Before Wilberforce could reply, they heard the sound of footsteps coming down the stairs. In one second flat, Wilberforce had wiped the chocolate off his face and leapt across to the doorway of the kitchen. Billy was only just sitting up by the time Mr and Mrs Bonkers came in.

"William Benedict Bertwhistle Bonkers!" said Mrs Bonkers with a gasp. "How could you?"

Billy opened and closed his mouth a few times. Everyone was staring at him and Mrs Bonkers folded her arms across her chest.

"You've eaten all the sweets!" she went on. "Oh, Billy! It's the day before Christmas Eve – there won't be any nice sweets left in the shops by now."

Billy looked around and saw that the washing machine door was open. A single sweet wrapper lay inside, and he picked it up. It was empty. "You hid them in the washing machine," he said.

"Well, I didn't think anyone else would dream of going there," said Mrs Bonkers, sounding extremely cross. "Wilberforce, what are you doing out of bed?"

Billy looked at Wilberforce and waited for him to own up. But Wilberforce just folded his arms and smirked.

"I came down to see if Billy was all right," he said. "I was worried when I saw he wasn't in bed."

Billy tried to say something, but it came out as a squeak.

"Not another peep out of you," said Mrs Bonkers. "Back to bed, everyone. We will think of a suitable punishment tomorrow!"

Billy got up late the next morning to find himself in disgrace. Mrs Bonkers put his bowl in front of him with an expression that said "marshmallow sparkle fudge whirls". Billy turned on the radio and spooned dry porridge oats into his mouth.

Usually, Billy was a boy who enjoyed his food. He liked eating and he was very good at it. But this morning, everything seemed wrong. Mrs Bonkers hadn't burnt the sausages in the way Billy liked. Mr Bonkers was too busy trying to teach Colin about football to pay attention to Billy. Great Uncle Herbert and Great Aunt Millie were hogging all the bacon, and Patricia was trying to get everyone to listen to excerpts from Wilberforce's latest school report.

"Now, back to the exciting news from the Town Hall this morning," squealed the radio breakfast-show presenter, Kylie Kickstart. *"No one here can believe Mayor Glutbucket's AMAZING announcement. For anyone who doesn't know — Mayor Glutbucket is offering a prize for the biggest snowman built this morning. Every kid in town can enter the competition*

to win a month's lip-smacking supply of your favourite sweets. It's like a snowman invasion in town, folks!

The deadline is two o'clock, so this is a great big shout-out to everyone under the age of sixteen. Get out in the snow and get building!"

Billy sat up straighter. Could it be true? Wilberforce smirked.

"You haven't got a chance," he whispered. "You've been snoring all morning – everyone else has already been building snowmen for hours. You snooze, you lose."

"You've just taken two extra rashers!" bellowed Great Uncle Herbert at his wife.

"Half past twelve, dear," replied Great Aunt Millie, clearly not listening.

"Madness!" Mr Bonkers exclaimed, waving his paper under Colin's nose. "Completely insane! He couldn't manage his way out of a paper bag, let alone the best football team in the world!"

"And his geography teacher actually used the phrase 'best pupil I have ever had'," said Patricia with a simper. Betty didn't answer, and it was at that moment Billy noticed his mother looking at him thoughtfully. She was wearing an expression that reminded him of the words "suitable punishment".

Something told Billy that it was time to make himself scarce. So he did something that he had never done before.

"I'm full," he said, pushing his bowl away. "I think I'll go for a walk."

There was a moment of shocked silence.

As I'm sure you know, extremely unlikely things do happen occasionally. Lightning sometimes strikes twice. Toast lands butter side up from time to time. But never before had Billy Bonkers left the table without finishing his meal.

"Do you feel ill, Billy?" asked Mrs Bonkers.

"I just want to go out," said Billy.

"But it's snowing, Billy," said Mr Bonkers. "Days like this are what sheds were invented for. I'm going to let off a test firework a bit later, if you want to join me."

Usually, Billy loved helping his dad in the shed. Letting off fireworks from inside a shed sounded like fun, and exactly the sort of thing Mrs Bonkers worried about. But at that moment, Billy didn't want to be around anyone else, not even his dad.

"I'll take my sledge," Billy muttered.

He trudged out of the kitchen, pulled on his coat and hat and grabbed his sledge from the hall.

"I don't know what's got into him," he could hear Mr Bonkers saying. "What has got into him? He's gone mad. My son has flipped his lid."

Soon Billy was dragging his sledge up the street and up the hill above the town. His tummy was growling in an unsatisfied sort of way and snow was whooshing up his trouser legs, but anything was better than being smirked at by Cousin Wilberforce.

"I would only have eaten one," he grumbled to himself. "Perhaps two. Not the whole lot!"

Billy wasn't a big fan of exercise. Watching football and playing computer games was enough for him. And by the time he was halfway up the hill, lugging a heavy sledge behind him, he had forgotten all about Wilberforce and the sweets. All he could think about was the snow inching up his trouser legs, and whether or not he would ever be able to stop panting.

Billy Bonkers

By the time he reached the top of the hill, Billy's legs were as wobbly as cooked spaghetti. He stopped and looked back. Far below, Christmas lights were twinkling in the town. If he half screwed up his eyes and slightly tilted his head, he could see a crowd of people in the town square. That must be where all the snowmen were being made. Soon the competition would be over and the winner would be taking home the prize of the year. Billy closed his eyes and imagined the month's supply of sweets that would never be his. He sighed, turned to pick up his sledge and... *slipped*.

It's Raining Sweets!

In rather a graceful manner, Billy flipped into the air, his legs pedalling as if riding an invisible bicycle. He was too surprised even to yell. He landed with a muffled thump on the soft snow, and for a moment he thought that everything was going to be all right.

That was when he started to roll.

Slowly at first, but steadily gathering speed, the portly form of William Benedict Bertwhistle Bonkers rolled down the snowy hill.

By now his trousers were tightly stuffed with snow, and as he rolled his woolly coat picked up more and more of it, packing tighter and tighter around him. The more snow he gathered, the rounder he became. And the rounder he became, the more snow he gathered. Billy was hurtling down the hill like a one-boy avalanche.

HEEELLLPPP!

Desperately, Billy aimed for anything he saw in his path, but nothing could stop him now. Branches, bottles and sticks and stones were swept up and packed tightly around Billy's body. He started to feel sick and closed his eyes.

At the bottom of the hill, the huge Billyball bounced once and bowled onto the road. Cars screeched out of his way as he rolled towards the town square.

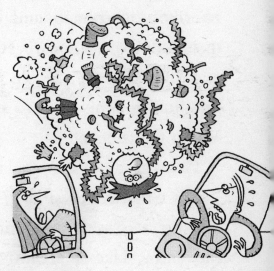

"HEEELLLPPP!" Billy

hollered.

More and more snow pressed around him, bringing with it lost coins, an old umbrella, several sprigs of mistletoe, seventeen chestnuts and a startling amount of tinsel.

Billy felt himself slowing down, and finally opened his eyes again. He was now rolling into the main square, past amazed children, enormous snowmen and alarmed grown-ups. Billy saw some of his schoolfriends and offered them a feeble smile. Then, with one final roll, he came to a stop in front of Mayor Glutbucket.

"Good gracious me!" exclaimed the Mayor.

Billy wriggled, twisted, jiggled and jerked, but he was well and truly stuck inside the snow. Like a gigantic white Weeble, he wibbled and wobbled himself into a standing position. Mayor Glutbucket's mouth fell open.

"Extraordinary!" he said.

Billy had turned himself into the strangest snowman anyone had ever seen. Tinsel had wound itself around his neck like a scarf. Twigs had made arms and an umbrella was pressed to his side. Best of all, the lost coins pressed all around his body were sparkling in the Christmas lights, making the Billy-snowman glitter and gleam.

Billy could hear a loud chattering sound, and after a moment he realised that it was his own teeth. He wiggled his fingers and pushed, and finally managed to get one hand free. He waved it at the Mayor, who shook his head and let out a rumbling chuckle.

"I am almost lost for words!" he cried. "I see before me the best, the most imaginative, the most dramatic snowman ever built! I declare that the winner of our Christmas competition is..."

He frowned and leaned closer to Billy to ask his name.

"B-B-B-Billy B-B-B-Bonkers," said Billy.

"BILLY BONKERS!" shouted the Mayor.

The main square erupted! Everyone was clapping and cheering. Cameras flashed and crowds of people gathered around, wanting to shake Billy's hand and ask him questions.

"How did you do it?"

"What was your inspiration?"

"Are you a genius?"

"I'm j-just an ordinary b-boy," said Billy with a modest shiver.

After cheers, applause, interviews and being pulled out of his snowman suit, Billy set off for home with a sack full of sweets. They gleamed and rustled in their shiny, colourful papers, and it wasn't easy to resist trying one of them, but he wanted to surprise his parents with the whole bag.

Billy Bonkers

When he reached his street it was getting dark, and neighbours were already arriving for the grand fireworks party. Billy could see Wilberforce opening the door and greeting them.

Just as Mr and Mrs Rocket reached the front door, there was a loud bang, followed by a sort of whooshing noise. Then Mr Bonkers' shed roof zoomed skywards in a shower of golden sparkles and red explosions.

"Oh cripes," said Billy. "There go Dad's fireworks."

Something must have gone wrong with the test firework. By the sound of it, Mr Bonkers had accidentally set off every firework he owned. The sky was a glittering mess of dazzling sparkles. Then Billy saw Mr Rocket chuckling. All the other neighbours were giggling too.

Everyone knew that Mr Bonkers had made a mistake.

"Don't laugh at my dad," muttered Billy.

So far, no one had spotted him. At that moment, the *Spider-Man* theme tune started playing in his head, and he sprang into action. Keeping his head down, Billy ran into next door's garden and scrambled over the fence into his own. He pressed his back against the house wall and edged his way towards the back door. Luckily, no one was in the kitchen. Down beside the shed, Mr Bonkers was hopping around and clutching his head with both hands.

Billy darted into the kitchen and peered into the hallway. Wilberforce was still standing at the front door, staring out at the fireworks. He had his back to Billy.

It's now or never, Billy thought, clutching the bag even more tightly.

He tiptoed along the hallway and up the stairs, hardly daring to breathe. All Wilberforce had to do was turn around and the whole plan would be ruined. But Billy reached his parents' room and dashed to the window. Most people had scrambled into the back garden, and were now watching open-mouthed as the shed exploded with rockets, bangers, shooting stars, Roman candles, crackling comets, screech rockets and spinners. No one was looking up at Billy.

He opened the window wide and then threw a handful of sweets out as hard as he could. He heard screams as they landed, and grinned to himself. Handful after handful of lollipops, fizzy bottles, acid drops and gobstoppers rained down on the party guests. The screams changed to squeals of excitement.

"Everyone, look!" he heard Mrs Furball shriek. "It's raining sweets!"

"What amazing fireworks!" shouted another voice.

"Roger Rocket's display was nowhere near as good as this!" cried someone else.

Billy grinned again, and started to throw even faster. When the sweets were all gone, he raced downstairs and slipped into the garden. Nobody noticed, although Mr Bonkers gave him a very curious look indeed.

"Wow, Dad, that was AMAZING!" Billy shouted. "It went PERFECTLY!"

He started clapping, and soon all the guests were clapping too. Mr Bonkers cleared his throat, scuffed the ground with his shoes and went rather pink.

"Mere trifle, mere trifle," he muttered.

"And that was just the start of the party, right, Dad?" Billy went on. "It's going to be a real Christmas cracker!"

Everyone cheered, and Mrs Rocket teetered up to Mr Bonkers on her highest heels.

"You're a party hero!" she said, batting her eyelashes and giving Mr Bonkers a peck on the cheek.

Mr Bonkers turned extremely pink, and Mr Rocket's eyes went a little bit bulgy.

"Everyone inside!" called Mrs Bonkers hastily. "It's far too cold to be standing around in skimpy party dresses."

As the guests trailed into the house, Mr Bonkers held onto Billy's collar and held him back.

"Billy, was that you?" he whispered. "How on earth did you do it?"

Billy shrugged.

"I just did the first thing that came into my head," he said.

As you probably know, Mr Bonkers wasn't the kind of man to gush with praise. He rubbed Billy's head a few times and put his hand on his shoulder.

"Tell you what, son," he said in a gruff voice. "We'll...er...forget all about that midnight sweet-eating. Least I can do, really. Saved my bacon tonight."

"No problem, Dad," said Billy, feeling very happy.

"Wouldn't be surprised if it had something to do with Wilberforce," Mr Bonkers added, tapping the side of his nose. "Bit of a plonker, that one."

Billy felt a lot better. He even felt a little bit sorry for Wilberforce. Yes, he was probably a genius and he might even end up on TV if his mother had anything to do with it. But Billy had something that Wilberforce could never, ever have.

The best dad in the world!

Up the Chimney!

It was Christmas Eve, and Billy Bonkers was worried. He had asked everyone, and one thing was obvious. He was the only person in the world who still hadn't sent a list to Father Christmas.

Wilberforce had written once a month ever since June.

Betty had sent her list at the beginning of December.

Even Great Aunt Millie had sent a letter up the chimney before she came to stay.

"That's the only sure and certain way to reach Father Christmas," she told Billy, tapping her stick on the floor to make her point. "Post can go missing, but the chimney will always send your letter straight to the North Pole."

Billy felt his heart sink into his slippers. The Post Office was now closed, and the Bonkers' chimney-less house was heated by a clanking old central-heating system.

Up the Chimney!

"NO," said Mr Bonkers, when Billy asked if they could install a chimney and a fireplace by midday.

Actually, Mr Bonkers said a lot more than that. He seemed to be under the impression that Billy had asked how central heating worked. Billy tried shaking his head and putting his hands over his ears, but nothing could quite drown out the explanation.

Unlike her husband, Mrs Bonkers understood exactly what Billy was asking. She clasped her hands and went pale.

"Lordy lorks, Billy, open fires are terribly dangerous! Goodness, I wouldn't be able to sleep a wink if we had one in the house. You and Betty could be burned to a crisp in your beds!"

Billy was willing to take that risk, but Mr and Mrs Bonkers folded their arms and said, "No," in unison.

"Fine," said Billy.

Of course, as I'm sure you understand, it wasn't fine at all. Relatives were occupying every chair in the sitting room, so Billy sat down on the bottom stair and cupped his chin in his hands. Betty was halfway up the stairs, reading a book called *50 Ways to Avoid Makeovers*. She glanced up from her page as Billy let out a loud groan.

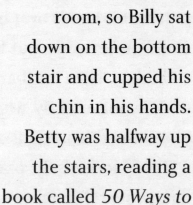

"I don't care about how the stupid central heating works," he said. "I just want the chimney."

"Whose chimney?" asked Betty, her eyes dropping to her book again.

Billy stared at her for a moment. Then he bounded up the stairs and gave her a hug.

"Of course! You're a genius, Betty Bonkers!"

"I know," said Betty. "Glad you've finally noticed."

"It doesn't have to be our chimney," Billy went on, grasping her shoulders in excitement. "Any chimney will do, right?"

"Direct line to Father Christmas," Betty confirmed. "But how are you going to find one?"

"Simple," said Billy. "I'll just look for a house with a chimney pot."

"Won't work," said Betty, still trying to read her book. "Loads of people have blocked off their chimneys from inside."

A strange feeling came over Billy. He usually only felt this level of focus and determination when food was involved. He clenched his fists, puffed up his chest and jutted out his chin. "I'm going to find a chimney and send that letter to Father Christmas by the end of the day, or my name's not Billy Bonkers!" he declared.

Billy began by making a list of all the houses on the street. He had been into most of them at one time or another, and he knew that they didn't have fireplaces. That left three houses that he had never visited.

He started with number nine. Like most of the houses in Billy's street on Christmas Eve, it was quiet. Everyone was snuggling into squashy chairs, watching their favourite films and eating too much. Billy tiptoed up to the house and squatted down underneath the sitting room window. He could hear the sound of a television. Hopefully, anyone inside would be looking at the screen. All he had to do was peep over the windowsill and check if there was a fireplace.

Inch by inch, Billy raised himself up and peered over the windowsill...

...straight into the bright blue eyes of a very, very surprised cat.

"MEEEOWWWCH!"

squawked the cat.

Inside the room (which didn't have a fireplace), two people leapt to their feet. Billy scrambled into a nearby rose bush for cover. He heard the front door flung open and a lot of shouting.

Billy groaned as quietly as he could. No fireplace here – just a bottom full of rose thorns.

The next house was number fifteen. There was a high fence all around the garden, and at first Billy couldn't think how to get inside. Then he discovered a small gap under the fence. By scooping out the earth, he managed to make a hole big enough to squeeze through.

The house and the garden needed a lot of work. The first thing that Billy noticed was the chimney...lying in an overgrown flowerbed.

G R R R O W L ...

For a moment Billy couldn't work out whether the sound was his groan of disappointment or his stomach rumbling.

Then he noticed the dog.

If you have a dog at home, you probably know that they are very special friends. A pet dog is always there to play with you, share your food, listen to your troubles and get hugely excited about sticks.

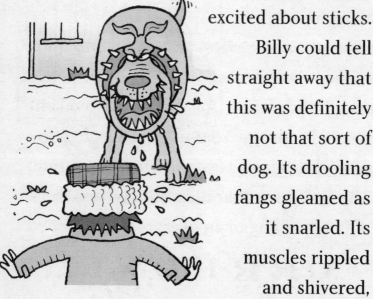

Billy could tell straight away that this was definitely not that sort of dog. Its drooling fangs gleamed as it snarled. Its muscles rippled and shivered, poised to spring forward. It was almost as tall as Billy, and it looked about three times as wide.

"G-g-good dog?" said Billy.

The dog let out a gurgling snarl that came from deep within its chest.

"Oh well," said Billy, using his most casual voice. "I can see that there's no working chimney here, so I'll just...er...be on my way."

There was a pause, and then Billy took a deep breath and dived for the hole under the fence. At the same moment the guard dog leapt through the air and fastened its jaws around the seat of Billy's trousers.

YAROOOWL!

The dog sprang back, its mouth full of rose thorns and trouser material. Clutching his bottom, Billy shot through the hole and filled it up as fast as he could. Then he sat down on the opposite side, panting, and listened to the dog hurling itself at the fence.

"I never knew hunting for fireplaces would be this dangerous," Billy said to himself.

The last house on his list was number twenty-three. It was an old building and it needed someone to take care of it. The windows were dirty

58

and cracked, the garden was full of weeds
and the green paint was peeling off
the door. Billy wondered what sort of
person lived there.

He was so interested in gazing up at
the house that he wasn't paying attention
to his feet. As I expect you know, that is
almost always a big mistake. This time was
no different. Suddenly there was nothing
underneath his foot. He wobbled, lost his
balance and fell
into a pond
with a
very loud
SPLASH.

"AARGH!" yelled Billy, feeling something wriggling up his trouser leg.

He was on his hands and knees in the pond, shaking out one leg behind him, when he heard someone shouting. An elderly man was standing on the veranda of the house, waving his walking stick at Billy.

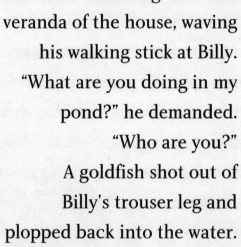

"What are you doing in my pond?" he demanded. "Who are you?"

A goldfish shot out of Billy's trouser leg and plopped back into the water.

Billy clambered out of the pond, dripping wet and shivering. He was so cold and shocked that he just blurted it out.

"I'm Billy Bonkers," he said, "and you've got a chimney! Does your fireplace still work? May I use it to send a letter to Father Christmas?"

The man's eyebrows knitted together in a fearsome frown.

"Christmas?" he roared. "PAH!"

"But this is my last chance," said Billy. "Please, Mr...er..."

"Scroggins," said the man. "Of course my fireplace works. And I'll let you use my chimney...the day I have a brain transplant and start giving a hoot about Christmas! Now clear off out of my garden!"

Billy squelched out of the garden and made his way home, thinking hard. Mr Scroggins was very grumpy and he obviously didn't think that Billy was going to take him seriously. But maybe that was exactly what he had to do. He had to make Mr Scroggins care about Christmas!

As Billy was walking home, he saw a group of Scouts carol-singing. They all looked very rosy-cheeked and happy. They didn't look like the sort of people who would have forgotten to write to Father Christmas. Billy glowered at them...and then suddenly a wonderful idea popped into his mind.

Now, Billy had never been a Scout. He had never even wanted to be a Scout. But he knew that they spent an awful lot of time doing Good Deeds.

"That's it!" he said to himself. "If I do a Good Deed for Mr Scroggins, he'll forget about being a grouch and let me use his chimney. Simple!"

Up the Chimney!

At home, Billy quickly changed into some dry clothes and put his ripped-up trousers into the bin. Then he hurried back to Mr Scroggins's house. The old man was walking gingerly down the snowy garden path.

He's going out! thought Billy. *This is my chance! Scouts are always helping old people to cross the road.*

"Don't worry, Mr Scroggins!" he said in a loud, cheerful voice. "I'll help you in all this slippy snow."

He took Mr Scroggins by the elbow and led him down the path and across the road. The old man seemed to be pulling away from him – he obviously didn't understand.

"Just lean on me, Mr Scroggins. I'll get you safely across the road."

He had to pull quite hard to get the old man onto the pavement on the other side of the road. Mr Scroggins was stuttering, probably overwhelmed by Billy's kindness. Billy held up his hand.

"No need to thank me, Mr Scroggins," he said in a cheerful voice. "If I could just use your fireplace for a minute..."

That was when he noticed that Mr Scroggins had gone purple.

"You blasted boy!" he bellowed. "Are you completely mad? Why have you dragged me over here?"

Billy started to get a niggling feeling that something wasn't quite right.

"I was just helping you cross the road," he said.

"I was only going to weed my garden!" Mr Scroggins snapped. "Pest of a boy!"

"Oh, sorry," said Billy, "I'll help you back across the road."

"Oh no you don't," said Mr Scroggins in a grumpy voice. "Clear off. I'm worn out with all this – I can't do my winter weeding now."

He shuffled back across the road and disappeared into his house, muttering about pests as he went.

Making a blooper like that would crush most people. But, as you know, Billy Bonkers was no ordinary boy. After all, he was the son of Mr Bonkers, and he knew that feeling embarrassed was a waste of valuable thinking time. Sure enough, another brilliant idea soon popped into his head.

If Mr Scroggins is too tired to do his weeding, I'll just have to do it for him, he thought. How hard can it be?

(Now, if you know anything about Billy Bonkers, you'll know that those were classic famous last words. And if you find it difficult to read about Very Embarrassing Mistakes, you should stop reading immediately and step away from this book.)

Billy crept into the garden and set to work. All the plants were covered with snow, but Billy guessed that it was the tallest ones that needed to be pulled out. His knees got wetter and wetter as he worked his way around the garden, pulling up all the weeds

by the roots. His hands were red and numb, but he just kept thinking about his letter to Father Christmas.

Billy had been working for about twenty minutes when he heard a banging sound and looked up. At first he couldn't figure out where the sound was coming from. Then he saw Mr Scroggins standing at his sitting-room window. He was banging on the glass, and he didn't look exactly grateful. Billy got an awful sinking feeling in the pit of his stomach as Mr Scroggins opened the window.

"What the blazes are you doing?" hollered the old man.

"Weeding!" replied Billy, holding up a handful of broken plants.

For a moment Mr Scroggins didn't seem able to speak. He spluttered and then

shouted, "Those are my favourite plants!"

Billy looked around at the garden. It was full of holes where he had pulled the plants out of the ground. Suddenly it looked more like a crime scene to Billy than a garden.

"Sorry, Mr Scroggins," he said. "I thought they were the weeds. Shall I put them back?"

"Clear off and leave my garden alone!" exclaimed the old man. "You've done enough!"

"Sorry," said Billy again.

He left the garden and sat down on the

pavement outside. Billy hadn't meant any harm, and he felt bad about Mr Scroggins's plants. But he was a Bonkers, and a Bonkers doesn't give up that easily.

"Maybe I should forget about Good Deeds and just think about Christmas," said Billy to himself. "I've got to think of a way to make Mr Scroggins feel Christmassy."

Then he remembered the Scouts he had seen singing carols.

"That's it!" cried Billy, leaping to his feet. "I'll sing to him!"

Billy ran up the steps to Mr Scroggins's veranda. He clasped his hands behind his back, took a deep breath and began.

Billy had sung "Jingle Bells" and "Good King Wenceslas", and was just starting "Ding Dong Merrily on High" when he heard an upstairs window open. He looked up...just in

time to see Mr Scroggins tipping a bucket
of icy water down
on him.

"No more
Christmas!"
he shouted.

Billy dripped his way
down the steps, out of the
garden and back to his
house. There was only one
thing left to do. He would
have to ask his sister for
help. Betty always seemed
to have a good idea or
two up her sleeve.

Billy went to change
out of his wet clothes. It was only when
he found Wilberforce sitting on his bed
that he remembered he was sharing his

room with his cousin. That made him feel even worse.

"You look a bit wet behind the ears," said Wilberforce with a snigger. "Haw haw haw."

Billy gritted his teeth. He hadn't forgotten that Wilberforce had let him take the blame for the sweet-snaffling.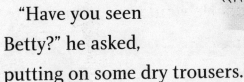

"Have you seen Betty?" he asked, putting on some dry trousers.

If there had been exams in snooping, Wilberforce would definitely have been top of the class.

"I think she's skulking around in the garden," said Wilberforce. "So why are you so wet?"

Billy pulled on a jumper with a large picture of Rudolph the Red-Nosed Reindeer on the front. Granny Bonkers had knitted it for him last Christmas, so it was rather tight, but it was the only one left in the drawer.

"See you later," Billy murmured. He left his room and went out to the garden. At first he couldn't see Betty anywhere, but then he saw the top of a pink bobble hat poking out from the other side of a holly bush. He tiptoed around it and found his sister sitting on an upturned bucket,

reading her book.
She jumped when
he tapped her on
the shoulder.

"Oh, I thought
you were Aunty
Abbie," she said.
"She's on a mission to
pluck my eyebrows."

"Betty, how can I cheer up an old man?"
asked Billy.

He explained everything that had
happened, hoping that his sister would
come up with a brilliant plan as usual. But
Betty shook her head.

"I'm sorry, Billy, I haven't got time to
think of a plan," she said. "It's taking all
my brainpower to think of ways to stop
Aunty Abbie from giving me a makeover.

I've managed to hide her beauty kit, but I bet she'll find it soon."

"But what about my letter to Father Christmas?" Billy asked with a groan.

"Well, it sounds to me as if Mr Scroggins has forgotten the spirit of Christmas," said Betty. "You just have to think of a way to remind him how Christmas used to feel when he was a little boy. What makes you feel Christmassy?"

Billy wandered off, thinking about Betty's question. What *did* make him feel Christmassy? His mum's food, definitely. Loud, happy music of course. And, obviously, loads of amazing presents. But what sort of present would a grumpy old man want?

He went back into the house and his nose led him to a plate of freshly baked mince pies in the sitting room. He slipped one into each pocket and began munching on a third. Great Uncle Herbert was telling Mr Bonkers a story about the old days.

"Ah, things were better then," said Great Uncle Herbert, slurping his tea. "A tin bath by the fire, my favourite comic and my best pal by my side. That's the trouble with kids today. They don't know how lucky they are."

He shot Billy a meaningful glance.

"So who was your best pal?" asked Billy, who didn't like the way this conversation was going.

"What was his name?"

"Patch," said Great Uncle Henry with a chuckle.

"Funny name for a boy," said Mr Bonkers. "Although I did go to school with a boy called Stinker Sidebottom."

Billy laughed and snorted a piece of mince pie up his nose.

"Patch wasn't a boy, he was a dog," said Great Uncle Henry. "Best dog in the world. My happiest memories are of playing with old Patch."

That's it! thought Billy. *I just have to remind Mr Scroggins what it felt like to be a little boy!*

With that, a beautiful and brilliant plan leapt into his head. He checked his watch.

Up the Chimney!

It was already ten past five. He had to get into town before the shops shut, and that meant he was going to have to run.

Now, Billy didn't run very often. He hardly ever even jogged. And sprinting was something that other people did on Sports Day. But to get his letter to Father Christmas, he was going to have to push himself to the limit.

Ten minutes later, Billy staggered into the pet shop, gasping for breath.

"Puppy," he wheezed. "I – need – a – puppy."

The owner was a short, plump lady with a smiley face. She held up one finger.

"I've got just one puppy left," she said. "His name is Clarence, and he's a little bit scruffy. Will that be all right?"

"That'll be perfect," said Billy.

Half an hour later, Billy was once again standing on Mr Scroggins's veranda. He had tied a scraggy piece of red tinsel around Clarence's neck. He had also pilfered one of Mrs Bonkers' special Christmas pork pies, the miniature tree and decorations from his bedroom, some silver bells and fairy lights from Betty's room and a portable CD player. He had even picked some holly branches from the bush in the garden. He was all set to turn the veranda into a magical Christmas grotto...

Billy draped the lights around the veranda, and then he realised that he didn't have anywhere to plug them in. He put the tree beside the front door, but suddenly it looked very sparse. There weren't enough holly branches, and there was no breeze to make the silver bells tinkle. Hoping that the music would make everything all right, Billy pressed the "Play" button.

The batteries must have been low, because instead of an upbeat Christmas rock song, it sounded like something that belonged at a funeral.

UHHHTS CHRUHHHSMUHHHS!

"What's that awful racket?" came a gruff voice from inside the house.

Heavy footsteps tramped towards the door. There was no time to run. Billy plonked

Clarence down in front of him and prepared to face his doom.

CREEEAK! The door opened slowly, and Mr Scroggins glared down at Billy and the puppy. His eyes widened as he took in the meagre tree and the non-working lights. His hand crept up to his head and grabbed a large handful of his own hair.

 "Are you mad, or am I?" he demanded. "What the blazes have you done to my porch?" Billy opened and closed his mouth several times, trying to think of the right thing to say.

"Don't just stand there doing goldfish impressions!" Mr Scroggins shouted. "Clear off home, and tell your parents to expect a visit from me!"

Up the Chimney!

Billy was about to shuffle away, but Clarence the puppy had other ideas. This was his big moment. After weeks of troublemaking in the pet shop, he wasn't about to slink off without making his mark.

He stood up, stretched lazily, raised an eyebrow and cocked his leg. An enormous wee arced through the air and splattered all over Billy's shoes.

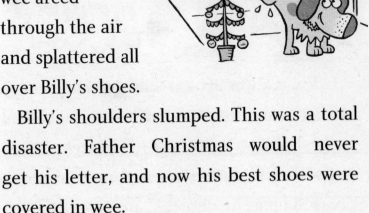

Billy's shoulders slumped. This was a total disaster. Father Christmas would never get his letter, and now his best shoes were covered in wee.

But as he squelched across the veranda, Billy heard something strange. It was a sort of snuffling, sniffling snort. He heard it again... and again. Billy looked up and saw that Mr Scroggins was shaking...with laughter.

"OOOH HOO HOO HOO! WAAAH HA HA HA! OHHH HEE HEE HEE!"

I don't know if you have ever seen an elderly man helpless with laughter. His belly shook so hard that his braces almost popped. His eyes streamed and his face creased up as he chortled and snorted.

"Oh!" he said eventually, his voice weak with laughter. "Oh! Oh! That's the funniest thing I've ever seen! That dog is a comedy genius!"

Mr Scroggins leaned against the doorpost, still shaking with helpless giggles.

"He's a present," said Billy in a small voice. "Happy Christmas, Mr Scroggins."

He picked up Clarence and put him into the old man's arms. The puppy reached up and licked his cheek.

For a moment, Mr Scroggins didn't say anything. When he spoke, his voice was as gruff as usual, but his eyes were very bright and shiny.

"What was it you wanted earlier?" he asked.

"Just to send a letter to Father Christmas up your chimney," said Billy, hardly daring to hope.

Mr Scroggins nodded a couple of times.

"Remember doing that myself, come to think of it,"
he said. "Well, hurry up. Haven't got all night."

Five minutes later, Billy's letter had disappeared up the chimney and Clarence was tucking in to a large fillet steak. Billy gathered his things from the veranda and said goodbye to Mr Scroggins. Then he squelched back down the road towards his house, feeling a great sense of relief.

All he had to do now was to be extra-specially good, right up until the moment that his presents were in his hands. That meant no practical jokes, lots of helping his mother and, above all, being nice to Cousin Wilberforce. Billy paused and thought for a moment.

The next few hours were going to be pretty tough...

Christmas Comedy Genius

Billy Bonkers was very good at sleeping.

He could sleep in the middle of the day. He could sleep sitting up. He could sleep upside down. (A talent he had discovered during a school project about bats.)

Once he had even fallen asleep while walking to school. He had only woken up when he tried to cuddle a lamppost.

Usually, Mr and Mrs Bonkers wanted Billy to get up. They hid alarms all around his room. They twirled football rattles next to his head. There was just one day of the year when everything went topsy-turvy.

On Christmas morning, Billy always woke up so early that the room was too dark to see if Father Christmas had been.

And this Christmas was no different.

Slowly, in the blackness, he reached down to the bottom of the bed, his fingers stretching out in front of him. Just when he thought that there was nothing there, his fingertips brushed against something bumpy, lumpy and crackly. It was his stocking, and it was crammed full of presents.

Dizzy with excitement, breathless and more awake than he had ever felt in his life, Billy tapped on the wall between his room and his parents' room.

"Can I open my stocking?"

For a moment, he thought that they hadn't heard him. Then he made out their sleepy, befuddled voices.

"Does he know what time it is?"

"The boy's gone mad."

"Go back to sleep, Billy."

"Not yet!"

If you have ever been in Billy's position, you will know that there is only one way to describe hearing those words on Christmas morning.

T O R T U R E !

He waited for as long as he could. At a rough guess, it was about three hours.

"Mu-um? Dad?"

"It's been ten minutes, Billy. Go back to sleep!"

Terrible doubts started to race through Billy's brain. What if Father Christmas hadn't got his letter in time?

What if the stocking was just a big trick by Wilberforce? I don't think anyone has actually exploded with anticipation on Christmas morning, but I can tell you that Billy was going the right way towards being the first.

"Mum! Dad! PLEASE!"

There was a squeak in his voice that his parents recognised. Mrs Bonkers sighed and turned on the bedside lamp. She looked at Mr Bonkers, who was trying to sit up and failing. He had also failed to open his eyes. "Merry Christmas, Sausage," Mrs Bonkers croaked.

92

Christmas Comedy Genius

Mr Bonkers made a noise in his throat. It could have been "Merry Christmas, Piglet". It could also have been "It was your idea to have children," or "Elf zombies eat pickles". By the time everyone was sitting around the table for Christmas lunch, twenty-five strong cups of tea had been made and drunk and Mrs Bonkers still had bags under her eyes. The sitting room had disappeared under a sea of wrapping paper and three toys had already been broken. (One of these was Wilberforce's new karaoke machine, and no one was trying very hard to fix it.)

The table was packed with food, and there was an absolutely enormous bowl of sprouts at the centre. As I expect you know, a lot of people hate sprouts. Not the Bonkers family. They were all mad about sprouts, and no one could cook a sprout quite like Mrs Bonkers. Last Christmas, Billy had put away eighteen sprouts, four helpings of turkey, twelve carrots, nine pigs in blankets and three ladlefuls of bread sauce. He was determined to beat his own record this year.

Billy had plate-piling down to a fine art. He started with a layer of roast potatoes, and then he fanned the pigs in blankets out around the edge of the plate to make even more room for food. Next he made rows of carrots and parsnips, followed by a layer of turkey slices. Next came a dollop of bread sauce and then some mashed potato. Sprouts were stuck into the mashed potato and sprinkled with tiny balls of stuffing. Dabs of cranberry sauce gave the final touch of colour. Then the whole thing was drenched in a splurge of thick gravy.

By now the food was piled so high that Billy couldn't see over it. His heart thumping with excitement, he adjusted his paper hat, raised his knife and fork, and began.

After the first few glorious mouthfuls of sprouty, potatoey, carroty goodness, Billy allowed himself to blink and breathe. Then he dived in again For a while, the only sound to be heard was gulping and swallowing, and the occasional fart from Great Uncle Herbert. Then, as people began to rest and relax between mouthfuls, they started to chat.

"I wonder what Father Christmas has for Christmas lunch," said Betty.

"Father Christmas is as nutty as a fruitcake," Mr Bonkers declared, waving his fork around with a slice of turkey on the end of it. "Mad to use reindeer when you could have a sports car. Don't tell me Father Christmas

wouldn't suit a big red sports car. Ultimate comfort! He's mad, I tell you."

"I can't wait to look at my present properly," Mrs Bonkers said, gazing longingly at her Top Hunks of the Year calendar.

Suddenly there was a loud pinging sound. Everyone stopped talking and looked up in surprise. Great Aunt Millie was hammering her dessert spoon against her glass.

"When I was a child, we always used to put on a performance after Christmas lunch," she said. "It would make an old lady very happy if the children could do the same today."

Billy and Betty exchanged horrified glances. Even Mrs Bonkers went a little pale. "Great Aunt Millie, I don't really think—"

"Oh, I shouldn't have asked," twittered Great Aunt Millie, pulling out a lace handkerchief and sniffing into it. "It's just an old lady's one Christmas wish. After all, I might not see another Christmas..."

Patricia leaned forward. She reminded Billy of a cat who had spotted a mouse.

"Performances?" she asked, licking her lips. "What sort of performances?"

"Recitals, riddles, that sort of thing," said

Great Aunt Millie. "I always used to sing, of course."

"Oh, Wilberforce, what a wonderful opportunity to show everyone your singing skills," said Patricia, clapping her hands together.

"I could sing and dance, Mummy," said Wilberforce.

"Er, I'm really not sure it's such a good idea," said Mr Bonkers, looking at Billy.

Billy could guess what his dad was thinking. He wasn't what you would call a natural dancer. In fact, when Billy started dancing, people usually got injured. But Patricia started to protest, and Great Aunt Millie's eyes filled with tears, and before Billy knew how, what or why, the unthinkable had happened. He had been roped into performing...in front of his entire family.

Billy tried really hard to think of a way to get out of it. He thought and thought. But whether it was the early morning start or the effect of twenty-five sprouts, his brain was on the sluggish side of normal.

"What are we going to do?" he hissed to Betty, while Colin was telling another cracker joke in a mystified voice. "You've got to think of something."

"I'm trying," said Betty.

Billy had a lot of respect for his sister's brain, so he popped another piece of turkey into his mouth and waited. Surely Betty could think up a way to get them out of this epic opportunity for humiliation?

After a few moments, Betty winked at him and dropped her knife on the floor.

"Oops, butterfingers!" she exclaimed, slipping under the table.

"I'll help you," said Billy, following her under the long red tablecloth.

Out of sight, Billy clutched his sister's shoulders.

"Tell me you've thought of a way out of this!"

"There is no way out of this," said Betty. "The best we can hope for now is to get through it without dying of humiliation."

Billy groaned and buried his face in his hands.

"We have to concentrate on something we're good at," said Betty. "I'll recite a poem off by heart, and you tell some jokes. You're always learning new ones from your joke books."

Billy felt a little bit better as he pulled himself back into his seat. After all, he did know a lot of jokes, and he still had half a plate of food and a bowl of Christmas pudding to enjoy before he had to perform.

How hard could it be?

After the plates had been scraped and the pudding had been scoffed, the grown-ups staggered into the sitting room. Great Uncle Herbert instantly fell asleep in one comfy chair, and Great Aunt Millie settled into the other one for the evening. Colin perched on a footstool, and Mrs Bonkers collapsed onto the sofa beside Patricia. Mr Bonkers lay down behind the sofa, clutched his stomach and did some groaning.

Billy waddled over to the
Christmas tree.
There were still
a few Christmas
chocolates dangling
from the branches,
and he was trying to
work out if he had
space for one when
Great Aunt Millie
waved her walking
stick at him.

"So," she said. "Who's going first?"

"Wilberforce," said Billy and Betty.

"Me!" said Wilberforce at the same time.

It was the first time the three of them had
agreed on anything. Wilberforce goggled at
Billy for a moment, and then raced upstairs
to get changed.

"That's agreed, then," said Mrs Bonkers, looking quite excited. "First Wilberforce, then Billy and then Betty. Ooh, it's going to be like a real talent show!"

"What jokes are you going to tell, Billy?" asked Betty.

Billy thought.

He thought some more.

He stopped, took a deep breath and thought even harder. Then he started to panic.

Billy had forgotten all his jokes! *Come on,* he told himself. *Think! Why did the chicken cross the road? Knock knock, who's there?*

But it was no good. He couldn't remember a single punch line. And let me tell you, if there's one thing more embarrassing than having to stand up and tell jokes in front of your entire family, it's forgetting those jokes in front of your entire family. There was only one thing for it. Billy was going to have to hide.

There weren't very many places in the house that weren't occupied by burping, farting or snoring relatives. In fact, there was only one place that Billy could think of – one place where no one would think to look. He went upstairs as fast as his belly would allow, and squeezed under Betty's bed.

Christmas Comedy Genius

Have you ever crawled under your sister's bed? If you have, you will know that it is a mysterious and alarming place. The Bonkers family only cleaned under the beds on special occasions, and Christmas wasn't one of them. Looking around, Billy found:

A five-pence piece  A hair bobble

A sparkly green comb

A holey sock

A scented rubber in the shape of a strawberry

A book called *Maths is Fun*

Half a mint
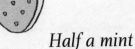

Billy blew the worst of the dust off the mint and popped it into his mouth. He wondered how long he would have to stay under there, and whether he would have to resort to eating the rubber. Then he saw a pair of feet come into the room and walk up to the bed. He knew that they were his sister's feet for two reasons. One, they were very bony, and two, she was wearing his socks. She was always stealing his socks.

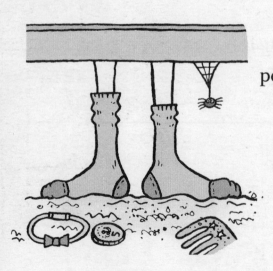

Betty knelt down and peered under the bed. "How did you know I was here?" gasped Billy.

"I'm a girl," said Betty. "Don't you think girls know when annoying brothers sneak into their room? Besides, I could hear you panting. Shouldn't have had that second dollop of clotted cream."

"Sock thief," Billy muttered, dragging himself out from under the bed.

"What's the matter?" Betty asked. "I thought you didn't mind the idea of telling jokes?"

Billy groaned and explained his memory-loss problem.

"Hmm, said Betty, putting her finger to her chin. "That is bad. It would be really embarrassing if you forgot the jokes in front of everyone. You'd have to change your name or run away to sea or something."

"I know that," Billy said. "What if I just say I won't do it? They can't make me. Not unless Dad's invented a new machine to force jokes out of me."

At that moment, they heard the high-pitched whine of the karaoke machine. Someone had got it working again. Then Wilberforce's reedy voice quavered around the house, accompanied by a loud banging noise. Billy and Betty rushed onto the landing and peered over the banisters. Wilberforce was in the door of the sitting room, wearing a black suit, a tartan bow tie and a pair of spats. He was tap dancing in time with the music. Billy couldn't see the rest of the family, but he could guess the  expression on his dad's face.

"We can't back out now," said Betty. "If we don't perform, Wilberforce will carry on singing all afternoon."

Billy shuddered, and knew that his sister was right. But how could he perform a joke routine with no jokes?

"I wish I could make my joke book invisible," he said. "Then I could take it with me and just read out the jokes, and no one would guess."

"Wait a minute!" Betty exclaimed. "I think I might have an idea. Maybe you can have an invisible joke book – sort of!" She raced into Billy's bedroom and grabbed a handful of his joke books. Then she beckoned Billy downstairs and led him out to Mr Bonkers' shed. Wilberforce was still dancing and singing at the top of his lungs, and as they walked to the shed, Billy glimpsed one of Mrs Furball's cats with its paws over its ears.

"I'm sure I remember seeing it here over the summer," Betty muttered, rummaging in a dark corner of the shed.

"Seeing what?" Billy asked.

"Aha," said Betty in a triumphant voice. "This!"

She held up Mr Bonkers' field radio kit. He had once dabbled with the idea of being a spy (mainly so that he could win competitions against Mr Rocket). After an incident involving the Girl Guides, a giant inflatable dolphin and a detective from Scotland Yard, he had given up, but he had never got rid of the equipment.

Betty pushed the earpiece into Billy's ear so that it couldn't be seen, and then spoke into the mic.

"CAN YOU HEAR ME?"

Billy jumped so hard that his head nearly hit the ceiling.

"Turn down the volume!" he said. "I'd like to keep my eardrums, please."

"Here's the plan," said Betty. "I'll sit here and read the jokes out to you, and you can repeat them. Simple!"

It really did sound very simple indeed. Billy should have known better, of course, but he was so used to Betty's plans working brilliantly that he didn't even question it. He hurried back to the house, waited for Wilberforce to finish tap dancing to his mum's favourite easy-listening tune, and then stepped out in front of his family.

"My name is Billy Bonkers," he began, "and I'm here to make you laugh until your socks fall off."

"Ok, let's go," said Betty's tinny voice in his ear. "Why did the chicken cross the road twice? Because he was a double-crosser."

Billy repeated the joke and there was a little ripple of laughter. So far, so good.

"Which dog can jump higher than a building?" Betty went on. "Any dog – buildings can't jump!"

Again Billy told the joke, and again everyone gave a little giggle.

It was when Billy was telling the sixth joke that things went wrong. He had just started to relax.

"What was the dinosaur doing in the fridge?" asked Billy.

Just as Betty was about to tell him the punch line, there was a sinister sort of crackle and everything went silent.

"I don't know," said Colin. "What was the dinosaur doing in the fridge?"

Billy tapped his ear a couple of times, and heard another faint crackle. Then a distant voice spoke, and Billy repeated the words without thinking.

"Asking for directions!"

Colin looked puzzled, but Mr Bonkers gave a loud snort of laughter and a stream of fizzy pop shot out of his nose. Mrs Bonkers started to giggle too.

Feeling desperate, Billy heard a joke and repeated it.

"What has thirty feet and sings?"

Again, the earpiece crackled and went silent. Panic-stricken, Billy had about three seconds to figure out the answer.

"A...thirty-foot tape measure...in a talent show," he said in a sudden rush.

There was something terribly wrong with the earpiece. If only they had checked it! Billy could have kicked himself, but he was too busy trying to piece together Betty's crackling words, not daring to sneak a glance at his audience.

Why do birds fly south in the winter? Because kangaroos eat bananas.

What's green with four legs? A seasick elephant on holiday.

What do cats eat in the Netherlands? Hamsterjam.

When Billy dared to look up, he gawped at his family. Mr Bonkers had gone bright red in the face and was crying with laughter. Mrs Bonkers was overcome by helpless giggles. Patricia and Colin were clinging to each other, weak with silent laughter. Great Uncle Herbert was making some very strange snorting noises, and even Great Aunt Millie was chuckling. Only Wilberforce looked puzzled. And for once, Billy was on his side. He really wasn't that funny. Was he?

"Absolute gobbledygook," hooted Mr Bonkers, wiping his eyes. "The best kind of comedy. My son, the comedy genius!"

The more gibberish Billy spouted, the more the grown-ups laughed and the more helpless they became. It was as if he was tickling them and they couldn't fight back. By the time he stopped, he had given up trying to listen to Betty's broken voice. He was just gabbling the first twaddle that came into his head, and his audience couldn't get enough of it. He saw Betty's head pop around the doorway. She beckoned to him.

The adults were so weak with laughter that he didn't think they could even hear him any more. So he shrugged his shoulders and followed Betty into the kitchen. Wilberforce was close behind him.

"What's got into them?" asked Wilberforce. "You were rubbish."

Billy had his faults, but dishonesty wasn't one of them. He laughed and shrugged.

"I know," he said. "Total baloney. Grown-ups have gone mad. No sense of humour."

"But why did they think it was so funny?" Wilberforce demanded.

Billy grinned and patted his cousin on the shoulder. It really had been a totally crazy Christmas, and this was the maddest thing yet. He actually felt friendly towards Wilberforce!

"Don't you get it?" he asked. "The grown-ups are all helpless and this kitchen is

crammed with food. Piles of it! Why are you wasting time asking questions? We'll probably never in our lives get another chance to eat this much lovely grub! Come on, Wilberforce, my friend…TUCK IN!"

THE END

If you liked

Billy Bonkers,

turn over for more

fantastically

funny stories!

Max and Molly's Guide To Trouble

Meet Max and Molly: terrorising the neighbourhood really extremely politely...

Max and Molly's guides guarantee brilliantly funny mayhem and mischief as we learn how to be a genius, catch a criminal, build an abominable snowman and stop a Viking invasion!

978 1 40830 519 5 £4.99 Pbk
978 1 40831 572 9 eBook

978 1 40830 520 1 £4.99 Pbk
978 1 40831 573 6 eBook

978 1 40830 521 8 £4.99 Pbk
978 1 408 31574 3 eBook

978 1 40830 522 5 £4.99 Pbk
978 1 408 31575 0 eBook

ORCHARD BOOKS
www.orchardbooks.co.uk